SCHOLASTIC JUNIOR CLASSICS

Doctor Dolittle

Retold from
Hugh Lofting
by Ellen Miles

SCHOLASTIC INC.

New York   Toronto   London   Auckland   Sydney
Mexico City   New Delhi   Hong Kong   Buenos Aires

Based on *Doctor Dolittle* by Hugh Lofting, which was first published in 1920.

Copyright © 2004 by Scholastic Inc.

ISBN 0-439-57425-0

12 11 10 9 8 7 6 5   6 7 8 9/0
Printed in the U.S.A.   40
First printing, January 2004

Contents

The First Chapter

Puddleby

ONCE upon a time, many years ago, when our grandfathers were little children, there was a doctor, and his name was Dolittle — John Dolittle, M.D. "M.D." means that he was a proper doctor and knew a whole lot.

He lived in a little town called Puddleby-on-the-Marsh. And whenever he walked down the street in his tall hat, everyone would say, "There goes the Doctor! He's a clever man." And the dogs and the children would all follow behind him, and even the crows that lived in the church tower would caw and nod their heads.

The house he lived in on the edge of the town was quite small, but it had a wide lawn with stone seats and weeping willows. His sister, Sarah, kept house for him.

The Doctor was very fond of animals and kept many kinds of pets. Besides the goldfish in the pond at the bottom of his garden, he had rabbits in the pantry, white mice in his piano, a squirrel in the linen closet, and a hedgehog in the cellar. He had a cow with a calf, too, and an old lame horse, and chickens, and pigeons, and two lambs, and many other animals. But his favorite pets were Dab-Dab the duck, Jip the dog, Gub-Gub the baby pig, Polynesia the parrot, and Too-Too the owl.

His sister used to grumble about all the animals and say they made the house untidy. And one day when an old lady with rheumatism came to see the Doctor, she sat on the hedgehog who was sleeping on the sofa and never came to see him again.

Sarah said, "John, how can you expect sick people to come and see you when you keep all these animals in the house? We are getting poorer every day. If you go on like this, none of the best people will have you for a doctor."

"But I like animals better than the 'best people,'" said the Doctor.

"You are ridiculous," said his sister, and she walked out of the room.

So, as time went on, the Doctor got more and more animals, and he had fewer and fewer patients. At last, he had only one patient left — Matthew Mugg, the Cat's-meat-Man, who didn't mind any kind of animal. The Cat's-meat-Man went around the streets of Puddleby with a tray full of meat stuck on skewers. People bought the meat for their cats and dogs. But the Cat's-meat-Man wasn't very rich and usually only got sick once a year. When he did, he paid the Doctor sixpence.

Sixpence a year wasn't enough to live

on, even in those long-ago days, and if the Doctor hadn't had some money saved up in his money box, no one knows what would have happened.

He kept on getting more pets and, of course, it cost a lot to feed them. And the money he had saved up grew littler and littler.

Then he sold his piano, and let the mice live in a bureau drawer. But the money he got for that, too, began to go.

And now, when he walked down the street in his tall hat, people would say to one another, "There goes John Dolittle, M.D.! There was a time when he was the best-known doctor in the west country. Look at him now. He hasn't any money and his stockings are full of holes!"

But the dogs and the cats and the children still ran up and followed him through the town — the same as they had done when he was rich.

The Second Chapter

Animal Language

ONE day, the Doctor was sitting in his kitchen talking with Matthew Mugg, the Cat's-meat-Man.

"Why don't you give up being a people's doctor, and be an animal doctor?" asked Matthew.

The parrot, Polynesia, was sitting in the window looking out at the rain and singing a sailor song to herself. She stopped singing and started to listen.

"You see, Doctor," Matthew went on, "you know all about animals — much more than any vet does. That book you wrote about cats — why, it's wonderful! You might have been a cat yourself. You know the way animals think. And listen:

You can make a lot of money doctoring animals. You see, I'd send all the old women who had sick cats or dogs to you. And all the farmers 'round about who had lame horses and weak lambs would come. Be an animal doctor."

When the Cat's-meat-Man had gone, Polynesia flew off the window onto the Doctor's table and said, "That man's got sense. That's what you ought to do. Be an animal doctor. Give the silly people up, if they haven't brains enough to see you're the best doctor in the world. Be an animal doctor."

"Oh, there are plenty of animal doctors," said John Dolittle, putting the flower-pots outside on the windowsill to get the rain.

"Yes, there *are* plenty," said Polynesia. "But none of them are any good at all. Now listen, Doctor, and I'll tell you something. Did you know that animals can talk?"

"I knew that parrots can talk," said the Doctor.

"Oh, we parrots can talk in two languages — people language and animal language," said Polynesia proudly. "If I say, 'Polly wants a cracker,' you understand me. But hear this: *'Ka-ka oi-ee, fee-fee?'*"

"Good gracious!" cried the Doctor. "What does that mean?"

"That means 'Is the porridge hot yet?' in bird language."

"My! You don't say so!" said the Doctor. "You never talked that way to me before."

"What would have been the use?" said Polynesia, dusting some cracker crumbs off her left wing. "You wouldn't have understood me if I had."

"Tell me some more," said the Doctor, all excited. He took up a pencil. "Now don't go too fast, and I'll write it down. Give me the birds' ABC's first — slowly now."

So that was the way the Doctor came to

know that animals had a language of their own and could talk to one another. All that afternoon, while it was raining, Polynesia sat on the kitchen table giving him bird words to write down.

At teatime, when the dog, Jip, came in, Polynesia said to the Doctor, "See, he's talking to you."

"Looks to me as if he's scratching his ear," said the Doctor.

"Animals don't always speak with their mouths," said Polynesia, raising her eyebrows. "They talk with their ears, with their feet, with their tails — with everything. Sometimes they don't *want* to make a noise. Do you see now the way he's twitching up one side of his nose?"

"What's that mean?" asked the Doctor.

"That means 'Can't you see that it has stopped raining?'" Polynesia answered. "He is asking you a question. Dogs nearly always use their noses for asking questions."

After a while, with Polynesia's help, the Doctor learned the language of the animals so well that he could talk to them himself and understand everything they said. Then he gave up being a people's doctor altogether.

As soon as the Cat's-meat-Man had told everyone that John Dolittle was going to become an animal doctor, old ladies began to bring him their pet pugs and poodles who had eaten too much cake, and farmers came many miles to show him sick cows and sheep.

One day, a plow horse was brought to him, and the poor thing was terribly glad to find a man who could talk in horse language.

"You know, Doctor," said the horse, "that vet over the hill knows nothing at all. He has been treating me six weeks now — for stiff joints. What I need is *spectacles*. But that stupid man over the hill never even looked at my eyes. He kept on giving me big pills. I tried to tell him, but he couldn't understand a word of horse language. I need spectacles."

"Of course — of course," said the Doctor. "I'll get you some at once."

"I would like a pair like yours," said the horse, "only green. They'll keep the sun out of my eyes while I'm plowing the field."

John Dolittle got a fine, big pair of green spectacles, and the plow horse stopped going blind in one eye and could see as well as ever.

And so it was with all the other animals that were brought to him. As soon as they found that he could talk their language, they told him where the pain was and how they felt and, of course, it was easy for him to cure them.

Now all these animals went back and told their brothers and friends that there was a doctor in the little house with the big yard who really *was* a doctor. And whenever any creature got sick — not only horses and cows and dogs, but all the little things of the fields, like harvest mice, water voles, badgers, and bats — they came to his house on the edge of the town. The Doctor's big yard was nearly always crowded with animals waiting to see him.

There were so many that came that he had to have special doors made for the different kinds. He wrote HORSES over the front door, COWS over the side door, and SHEEP on the kitchen door. Even the mice had a tiny tunnel made for them into the cellar, where they waited patiently in rows for the Doctor to come around to them.

And so, in a few years' time, every living thing for miles and miles knew about John Dolittle, M.D. And the birds who flew to other countries in the winter told the animals in foreign lands of the wonderful doctor of Puddleby-on-the-Marsh, who could understand their talk and help them in their troubles. In this way, he became famous among animals all over the world, better known even than he had been among the folks of the west country. And he was happy and liked his life very much.

One afternoon when the Doctor was busy writing in a book, Polynesia sat in the window — as she nearly always did — looking out at the leaves blowing about in the garden. Suddenly, she laughed aloud.

"What is it, Polynesia?" asked the Doctor, looking up from his book.

"I was just thinking about people," said Polynesia. "They think they're so wonderful. But the world has been going on now for thousands of years, hasn't it? And the only thing in animal language that *people* have learned to understand is that when a dog wags his tail he means 'I'm glad!' It's funny, isn't it? You are the very first man to talk like us. People are always talking about 'the dumb animals.' *Dumb*! Huh! Why, I knew a macaw once who could say

'Good morning!' in seven different languages and knew more geography than people will ever know. *People!* Golly! I suppose if people ever learn to fly — like any common hedge sparrow — we shall never hear the end of it!"

"You're a wise old bird," said the Doctor. "How old are you really? I know that parrots and elephants sometimes live to be very, very old."

"I can never be quite sure of my age," said Polynesia. "It's either a hundred and eighty-three or a hundred and eighty-two." Then she fluffed her feathers proudly and went back to watching the leaves.

The Third Chapter

More Money Troubles

SOON the Doctor began to make money again and his sister, Sarah, was happy.

Some of the animals who came to see him were so sick that they had to stay at the Doctor's house for a week. And often even after they got well, they did not want to go away — they liked the Doctor and his house so much. And he never had the heart to refuse them when they asked if they could stay with him. So, in this way, he went on getting more and more pets.

One evening, an organ grinder came around with a monkey on a string. The Doctor saw that the monkey's collar was too tight and that he was dirty and unhappy. So he took the monkey away from the man. He gave the man a shilling and told him to go. The organ grinder got awfully angry and said that he wanted to keep the monkey. But the Doctor told him that if he didn't go away, he would punch him on the nose. John Dolittle was a strong man, though he wasn't very tall. So the man went away saying rude things, and the monkey stayed with Doctor Dolittle and had a good home. The other animals in the house called him Chee-Chee, which is a common word in monkey language, meaning "ginger."

Another time, when the circus came to Puddleby, a crocodile who had a bad toothache escaped at night and came to see the Doctor. The Doctor talked to him in crocodile language and took him into the house and made his tooth better. But when the crocodile saw what a nice house it was, he wanted to stay. He asked if he could sleep in the fishpond at the bottom of the garden if he promised not to eat the fish. When the circus men came to take him back he got so wild and savage that he frightened them away. But to everyone in the house he was always as gentle as a kitten.

But now the old ladies grew afraid to send their lapdogs to Doctor Dolittle because of the crocodile, and the farmers wouldn't believe that he would not eat the lambs and sick calves they brought to be cured. So the Doctor went to the crocodile and told him he must go back to his circus. But he wept such big tears, and begged so hard to be allowed to stay, that the Doctor didn't have the heart to turn him out.

So then Sarah said, "John, you must send that creature away. Now the farmers and the old ladies are afraid to send their animals to you — just as we were beginning to be well off again. We shall be ruined entirely. This is the last straw. I will no longer be your housekeeper if you don't send away that alligator."

"It isn't an alligator," said the Doctor, "it's a crocodile."

"I don't care what you call it," said Sarah. "It's a nasty thing to find under the bed. I won't have it in the house."

"But he has promised me," the Doctor answered, "that he will not bite anyone. He doesn't like the circus, and I don't have the money to send him back to Africa where he comes from. He minds his own business and, on the whole, is very well behaved."

"I tell you I will *not* have him around," said Sarah. "He eats the linoleum. If you don't send him away this minute, I'll leave myself!"

"All right," said the Doctor, "go ahead. It can't be helped."

So Sarah Dolittle packed up her things

and went off, and the Doctor was left all alone with his animal family.

And very soon he was poorer than he had ever been before. With all those mouths to fill, and the house to look after, and no money coming in to pay the butcher's bill, things began to look very bleak. But the Doctor didn't worry at all.

"Money is a nuisance," he would say. "We'd all be much better off if it had never been invented. What does money matter, so long as we are happy?"

But soon the animals themselves began to get worried. One evening when the Doctor was asleep in his chair by the kitchen fire, they began talking it over among themselves in whispers. The owl, Too-Too, who was good at arithmetic, figured out that there was only enough money to last another week — if they each had one meal a day and no more.

Then Polynesia said, "I think we all ought to do the housework ourselves. At least we can do that much. After all, it is for our sakes that the old man finds himself so lonely and so poor."

So it was agreed that the monkey, Chee-Chee, was to do the cooking and mending; the dog, Jip, was to sweep the floors; Dab-Dab the duck was to dust and make the beds; the owl, Too-Too, was to keep the accounts; and little Gub-Gub the pig was to do the gardening. They made Polynesia housekeeper and laundress, because she was the oldest.

Of course, at first, they all found their new jobs very hard to do — all except Chee-Chee, who had hands, and could do things like a man. But they soon got used to it, and they found it such fun to watch Jip sweeping his tail over the floor with a rag tied onto it for a broom. After a little while, they learned to do the work so well that the Doctor said he had never had his house kept so tidy or so clean before.

In this way, things went along all right

for a while, but without money they could not pay all the bills. But still the Doctor wouldn't worry. When Polynesia came to the Doctor and told him that the fishmonger wouldn't give them any more fish, he said, "Never mind. As long as the hens lay eggs and the cow gives milk, we can have omelettes and pudding. And there are plenty of vegetables left in the garden. Winter is still a long way off."

But the snow came earlier than usual that year. The old lame horse hauled in plenty of wood from the forest outside the town, so they could have a big fire in the kitchen. But most of the vegetables in the garden were gone, and the rest were covered with snow, and many of the animals were really hungry.

The Fourth Chapter

A Message from Africa

THAT winter was a very cold one. One night, the animals were all sitting around the warm fire in the kitchen listening to the Doctor reading aloud. Too-Too suddenly said, "Shh! What's that noise outside?"

The door flew open and Chee-Chee ran in, badly out of breath.

"Doctor!" he cried, "I've just had a message from a cousin of mine in Africa. There is a terrible sickness among the monkeys there. They are all catching it — and they are dying by the hundreds. They have heard of you, and beg you to come to Africa to stop the sickness."

"Who brought the message?" asked the Doctor, laying down his book.

"A swallow," said Chee-Chee. "She is waiting outside."

"Bring her in by the fire," said the Doctor. "She must be perished with the cold."

So the swallow was brought in, all huddled and shivering. She was a little afraid at first, but she soon got warmed up and sat on the edge of the mantelpiece and began to talk.

When she had finished, the Doctor said, "I would gladly go to Africa — especially in this bitter weather. But I'm afraid we haven't money enough to buy the tickets. Get me the money box, Chee-Chee."

So the monkey climbed up and got it off the top shelf of the dresser. There was nothing in it — not one single penny!

"I felt sure there was twopence left," said the Doctor.

"There was," said Too-Too. "But you spent it on a rattle for that badger's baby when he was teething."

"Did I?" said the Doctor, "Dear me, dear me! What a nuisance money is, to be sure! Well, never mind. Perhaps I shall be able to borrow a boat that will take us to Africa. I knew a seaman once whose baby I cured of the measles. Maybe he'll lend us his boat."

So early the next morning, the Doctor went down to the seashore. And when he came back, he told the animals that the sailor was going to lend them the boat.

Then the crocodile and Chee-Chee and Polynesia were very glad and began to sing, because they were going back to Africa, their real home. And the Doctor said, "I shall only be able to take you three — and Jip, Dab-Dab, Gub-Gub, and Too-Too. The rest of the animals, like the squirrels and the water voles and the bats, will have to go back and live in the fields. But most of them sleep through the winter, so they won't mind."

Polynesia, who had been on long sea

voyages before, began telling the Doctor all the things he would have to take on the ship. "You must have plenty of sea biscuits," she said. "'Hardtack' they call it. And you must have beef in cans — and an anchor."

"I expect the ship will have its own anchor," said the Doctor.

"Well, make sure," said Polynesia. "Because it's very important. You can't stop if you haven't got an anchor. And you'll need a bell."

"What's that for?" asked the Doctor.

"To tell the time by," said Polynesia. "You go and ring it every half hour and then you know what time it is. And bring a whole lot of rope — it always comes in handy on voyages."

Then they began to wonder where they were going to find the money to buy all the things they needed.

"Oh, bother! Money again," cried the Doctor. "Goodness! I'll go ask the grocer if he will wait for his money till I get back. No, I'll send the sailor to ask him."

So the sailor went to see the grocer and came back with all the things they wanted.

Then the animals packed up and closed the house and gave the key to the old horse who lived in the stable. And when they had seen that there was plenty of hay in the loft to last the horse through the winter, they carried all their luggage down to the seashore and got onto the boat.

As soon as they were on the ship, Gub-Gub asked where the beds were, for it was four o'clock in the afternoon, and he wanted his nap. He was still a baby, after all. So Polynesia took the little pig downstairs into the ship and showed him the beds, set all on top of one another like bookshelves against a wall.

"Why, that isn't a bed!" cried Gub-Gub. "That's a shelf!"

"Beds are always like that on ships,"

said Polynesia. "Climb up into it and go to sleep. That's what you call a 'bunk.'"

"I don't think I'll go to bed yet," said Gub-Gub. "I'm too excited. I want to go upstairs again and see them start."

"Well, this is your first trip," said Polynesia. "You will get used to the life after a while." And she went back up the stairs of the ship, singing this song to herself:

I've seen the Black Sea and the Red Sea;
  I rounded the Isle of Wight;
I discovered the Yellow River,
  And the Orange, too — by night.
Now Greenland drops behind again,
  And I sail the ocean blue.
I'm tired of all these colors, Jane,
  So I'm coming back to you.

They were just going to start on their journey when the Doctor said he would have to go back and ask the sailor the way to Africa. But the swallow said she had been there many times and would show them the way.

So the Doctor told Chee-Chee to pull up the anchor, and the voyage began.

The Fifth Chapter

The Long Journey

FOR six whole weeks they went sailing on and on, over the rolling sea, following the swallow. At night she carried a tiny lantern, so they would not miss her in the dark. People on the other ships that passed said that the light must be a shooting star.

As they sailed farther and farther south, it got warmer and warmer. Polynesia, Chee-Chee, and the crocodile enjoyed the hot sun. But Gub-Gub and Jip and Too-Too could do nothing in such weather. The pig and the dog and the owl sat in the shade of a big barrel with their tongues hanging out, drinking lemonade.

Dab-Dab kept herself cool by jumping

into the sea and swimming behind the ship. And every once in a while, when the top of her head got too hot, the duck would dive under the ship and come up on the other side.

When they got near the equator, they saw some flying fishes coming toward them. The fishes asked Polynesia if this was Doctor Dolittle's ship. When she told them it was, they said they were glad, because the monkeys in Africa were getting worried that he would never come. Polynesia asked them how many miles they had yet to go, and the flying fishes said it was only fifty-five miles now to the coast of Africa.

One evening soon after that, as the sun was going down, the Doctor said, "Get me the telescope, Chee-Chee. Very soon we should be able to see the shores of Africa."

And about half an hour later, sure enough, they thought they could see something in front that might be land. But it began to get darker and darker and they couldn't be sure. Then a huge storm blew in, with thunder and lightning. The wind howled, the rain came pouring down, and the waves got so high, they splashed right over the boat.

Then there was a big bang! The ship stopped and rolled over on its side.

"What happened?" asked the Doctor, coming up from downstairs.

"I'm not sure," said Polynesia, "but I think we're shipwrecked. Tell Dab-Dab to get out and see."

So Dab-Dab dived right down under the waves. And when she came up she said they had struck a rock. There was a big hole in the bottom of the ship, the water was coming in, and they were sinking fast.

"We must have run into Africa," said the Doctor. "Dear me, dear me! Well, we must all swim to land."

But Chee-Chee and Gub-Gub did not know how to swim.

"Get the rope!" said Polynesia. "I told you it would come in handy. Where's that duck? Come here, Dab-Dab. Take this end of the rope, fly to the shore, and tie it onto a palm tree. We'll hold the other end on the ship here. Then those that can't swim must climb along the rope till they reach the land. That's what you call a 'lifeline.'"

So they all got safely to the shore — some swimming, some flying. Those that climbed along the rope brought the Doctor's trunk and medicine bag with them.

But the ship was no good anymore with the big hole in the bottom. The rough sea beat it to pieces on the rocks and the timbers floated away.

Then they all took shelter in a nice dry cave they found, high up in the cliffs, till the storm was over.

When the sun came out the next morning, they went down to the sandy beach to dry themselves.

"Dear old Africa!" sighed Polynesia. "It's good to be back. Just think — it'll be a hundred and sixty-nine years tomorrow since I was here! And it hasn't changed a bit! Same old palm trees, same red earth. There's no place like home!"

And the others noticed she had tears in her eyes. She was so pleased to see her home once again.

Chee-Chee suddenly said, "Shh! I hear footsteps in the jungle!"

They all stopped talking and listened. And soon a tall man came down out of the woods and asked them what they were doing there.

"My name is John Dolittle, M.D.," said the Doctor. "I have been asked to come to Africa to cure the monkeys who are sick."

"You must all come before the King," said the man.

"What king?" asked the Doctor, who didn't want to waste any time.

"The King of the Jolliginki," the man answered. "All these lands belong to him, and all strangers must be brought before him. Follow me."

So they gathered up their baggage and went off, following the man through the jungle.

The Sixth Chapter

Polynesia and the King

WHEN they had gone a little way through the thick forest, they came to a wide, clear space, and they saw the King's palace, which was made of mud.

This was where the King lived with his Queen, Ermintrude, and their son, Prince Bumpo. The Prince was away fishing for salmon in the river. But the King and Queen were sitting under an umbrella before the palace door.

The King asked the Doctor his business, and the Doctor told him why he had come to Africa.

"You may not travel through my lands," said the King. "Many years ago a white man came to these shores, and I was very kind to him. But after he had dug holes in the ground to get the gold, and killed all the elephants to get their ivory tusks, he went away secretly in his ship — without so much as saying thank you. Never again shall a white man travel through the lands of Jolliginki."

Then the King turned to some of the men who were standing near and said, "Take away this medicine man with all his animals, and lock them up in my strongest prison."

So six of the men led the Doctor and all his pets away and shut them up in a stone dungeon. The dungeon had only one little window, high up in the wall, with bars in it, and the door was strong and thick.

The animals all got very sad, and Gub-Gub began to cry. But Chee-Chee said he would spank him if he didn't stop that horrible noise, and so the baby pig kept quiet.

"Are we all here?" asked the Doctor, after he had got used to the dim light.

"Yes, I think so," said Dab-Dab and started to count them.

"Where's Polynesia?" asked the crocodile. "She isn't here."

"Are you sure?" said the Doctor. "Look again. Polynesia! Polynesia! Where are you?"

"I suppose she escaped," grumbled the crocodile. "Well, that's just like her! Sneaking off into the jungle as soon as her friends get into trouble."

"I'm not that kind of a bird," said the parrot, climbing out of a pocket in the Doctor's coat. "You see, I'm small enough to get through the bars of that window, and I was afraid they would put me in a cage instead. So while the King was busy talking, I hid in the Doctor's pocket — and here I am!"

"Good gracious!" cried the Doctor. "You're lucky I didn't sit on you."

"Now listen," said Polynesia. "Tonight, as soon as it gets dark, I am going to creep

36

through the bars of that window and fly over to the palace. And then — you'll see — I'll soon find a way to make the King let us all out of prison."

"Oh, what can *you* do?" said Gub-Gub, turning up his nose and beginning to cry again. "You're only a bird!"

"Quite true," said Polynesia. "But do not forget that although I am only a bird, I can talk like a man — and I am really quite clever."

So that night, when the moon was shining through the palm trees and all the King's men were asleep, the parrot slipped out through the bars of the prison and flew across to the palace. She went in through a pantry window. Then she tiptoed up the stairs till she came to the King's bedroom. She opened the door gently and peeped in.

Queen Ermintrude was away at a dance that night, but the King was in bed, fast asleep.

Polynesia crept in, very softly, and got under the bed.

Then she coughed — just the way Doctor Dolittle coughed. Polynesia could mimic anyone.

The King opened his eyes and said sleepily, "Is that you, Ermintrude?"

Then Polynesia coughed again — loud, like a man. The King sat up, wide awake, and said, "Who's that?"

"I am Doctor Dolittle," said Polynesia — just the way the Doctor would have.

"What are you doing in my bedroom?" cried the King. "How dare you escape from prison! Where are you? I don't see you."

But Polynesia just laughed — a long, deep, jolly laugh, like the Doctor's.

"Stop laughing and come here at once, so I can see you," said the King.

"Foolish King!" answered Polynesia. "Have you forgotten that you are talking to John Dolittle, M.D., the most wonderful man on earth? Of course you cannot see me. I have made myself invisible. There is nothing I cannot do. Now listen: I have come here tonight to warn you. If you don't let me and my animals travel through your kingdom, I will make you and all your people sick like the monkeys. For I can make people well, and I can make people ill — just by raising my little finger. Send your soldiers at once to open the dungeon door, or you shall have mumps before the morning sun has risen on the hills of Jolliginki."

Then the King began to tremble and was very much afraid. "Doctor," he cried, "it shall be as you say. Do not raise your little finger, please!" And he jumped out of bed and ran to tell the soldiers to open the prison door.

As soon as he was gone, Polynesia crept downstairs and left the palace by the pantry window.

But the Queen, who was just letting herself in the back door with a latchkey, saw the parrot going out. And when the King came back to bed she told him what she had seen.

Then the King understood that he had been tricked, and he was dreadfully angry. He hurried back to the prison at once.

But he was too late. The door stood open. The dungeon was empty. The Doctor and all his animals were gone.

The Seventh Chapter

The Bridge of Apes

QUEEN Ermintrude had never in her life seen her husband so terrible as he was that night. He gnashed his teeth with rage. He called everybody a fool. He threw his toothbrush at the palace cat. He rushed around in his nightshirt and woke up his army and sent them into the jungle to catch the Doctor. Then he made all his servants go, too — his cooks and his gardeners and his barber and Prince Bumpo's tutor. Even the Queen, who was tired from dancing in a pair of tight shoes, was packed off to help the soldiers in their search.

All this time, the Doctor and his animals were running through the forest toward the Land of the Monkeys, as fast as they could go.

Gub-Gub, with his short legs, soon got tired, and the Doctor had to carry him — which was pretty hard, since he had the trunk and the medicine bag with him as well.

The King of the Jolliginki thought it would be easy for his army to find them, because the Doctor was in a strange land and would not know his way. But he was wrong, because Chee-Chee knew all the paths through the jungle — better even than the King's men did. Chee-Chee led the Doctor and his pets to the very thickest part of the forest — a place where no man had ever been before — and they all hid in a big hollow tree between high rocks.

"We had better wait here," said Chee-Chee, "till the soldiers have gone back to bed. Then we can go on to the Land of the Monkeys."

So there they stayed the whole night through.

They often heard the King's men searching and talking in the jungle nearby. But they were quite safe, for no one knew of that hiding place except Chee-Chee — not even the other monkeys.

At last, when daylight began to come through the thick leaves overhead, they heard Queen Ermintrude saying in a very tired voice that it was no use looking any more — that they might as well go back and get some sleep.

As soon as the soldiers had all gone home, Chee-Chee brought the Doctor and his animals out of the hiding place, and they set off for the Land of the Monkeys.

It was a long, long way, and they often got very tired — especially Gub-Gub. But when he cried, they gave him milk out of the coconuts, which he was very fond of.

They always had plenty to eat and

drink, because Chee-Chee and Polynesia knew all the different kinds of fruits and vegetables that grow in the jungle — like dates and figs and groundnuts and ginger and yams — and where to find them. They made their lemonade out of the juice of wild lemons, sweetened with honey that they got from the bees' nests in hollow trees.

At night, they slept in tents made of palm leaves, on thick, soft beds of dried grass. And after a while, they got used to walking a lot and did not get so tired and enjoyed the life of travel very much.

But they were always glad when night came and they stopped for their resting time. Then the Doctor would make a little fire of sticks, and after they had eaten their supper, they would sit around it in a ring, listening to Polynesia singing songs about the sea, or to Chee-Chee telling stories of the jungle.

Many of the tales that Chee-Chee told

were very interesting. Although the monkeys have no history books of their own, they remember everything that happens by telling stories to their children. Chee-Chee told tales of long, long, long ago, of the days when men dressed in bearskins and lived in holes in the rocks. And he told them of the great mammoths and lizards, as long as a train, that wandered over the mountains in those times, nibbling from the treetops.

When the King's army had gone back and told the King that they couldn't find the Doctor, the King sent them out again and told them they must stay in the jungle till they caught him. So all this time, while the Doctor and his animals were going along toward the Land of the Monkeys thinking themselves quite safe, they were still being followed by the King's men. If Chee-Chee had known this, he most likely would have hidden them again. But he didn't know it.

One day, Chee-Chee climbed up a high rock and looked out over the treetops. When he came down, he said they were now quite close to the Land of the Monkeys and would soon be there.

That same evening, sure enough, they saw Chee-Chee's cousin and a lot of other monkeys, who had not yet gotten sick, sitting in the trees by the edge of a swamp, looking and waiting for them. And when they saw the famous doctor, these monkeys made a tremendous noise, cheering and waving leaves and swinging out of the branches to greet him.

They wanted to carry his bag and his trunk and everything he had. One of the bigger ones even carried Gub-Gub. Then two of them rushed on in front to tell the sick monkeys that the great doctor had come at last.

But the King's men, who were still following, heard the noise of the monkeys cheering, too, and they at last knew where the Doctor was, and hurried on to catch him.

The big monkey carrying Gub-Gub was following along behind slowly, and he saw the captain of the army sneaking through the trees. So he hurried after the Doctor and told him to run.

Then they all ran harder than they had ever run in their lives. The King's men, coming after them, began to run, too.

Finally, Chee-Chee shouted, "It's all right! We don't have far to go now!"

But before they could get to the Land of the Monkeys, they came to a steep cliff with a river flowing below. This was the end of the Kingdom of Jolliginki, and the Land of the Monkeys was on the other side — across the river.

Jip looked down over the edge of the steep, steep cliff and said, "Golly! How are we ever going to get across?"

"Oh, dear!" said Gub-Gub. "The King's men are quite close now. Look at them! I am afraid we are going to be taken back to prison again." And he began to weep.

But the big monkey who was carrying the pig dropped him on the ground and cried out to the other monkeys. "Boys — a bridge! Quick! Make a bridge! We've only a minute to do it. Get lively! A bridge! A bridge!"

The Doctor began to wonder what they were going to make a bridge out of, and he gazed around to see if they had any boards hidden nearby.

But when he looked back at the cliff, there, hanging across the river, was a bridge all ready for him — made of living monkeys! For while his back was turned, the monkeys — quick as a flash — had made themselves into a bridge, just by holding hands and feet.

The big one shouted to the Doctor, "Walk over! Walk over — all of you — hurry!"

Gub-Gub was a bit scared, walking on

such a narrow bridge at that dizzying height above the river. But he got over all right, and so did all of them.

John Dolittle was the last to cross. And just as he was getting to the other side, the King's men came rushing up to the edge of the cliff.

They shook their fists and yelled with rage, for they saw they were too late. The Doctor and all his animals were safe in the Land of the Monkeys, and the bridge was pulled across to the other side.

Then Chee-Chee turned to the Doctor and said, "Many great explorers have spent long weeks hidden in the jungle waiting to see the monkeys do that trick. But we never let a foreign man get a glimpse of it before. You are the first to see the famous 'Bridge of Apes.'"

And the Doctor felt very pleased.

The Eighth Chapter

Curing the Monkeys

JOHN Dolittle now became dreadfully, awfully busy. He found hundreds and thousands of monkeys sick — gorillas, orangutans, chimpanzees, dog-faced baboons, marmosets, gray monkeys, red ones — all kinds. And many had died.

The first thing he did was to separate the sick ones from the well ones. Then he got Chee-Chee and his cousin to build him a little house of grass. Next, he vaccinated all the monkeys who were still well.

For three days and three nights, the monkeys kept coming from the jungles and the valleys and the hills to the little house of grass, where the Doctor sat all day and all night, vaccinating and vaccinating.

Then he had another house made — a big one, with a lot of beds in it — and he put all the sick ones in this house.

But so many were sick, there were not enough well ones to do the nursing. So the Doctor sent messages to the other animals, asking them to come and help with the nursing.

The Leader of the Lions got the message, but he was a very proud creature. He thought that nursing "a lot of dirty monkeys" was beneath the King of Beasts. But his wife convinced him that the Doctor was a good man who deserved help, and soon the Leader of the Lions had rounded up not only all the lions, but the leopards and the antelopes, too. There were so many of them that the Doctor had to send some away, and only kept the cleverest.

And very soon the monkeys began to get better. At the end of a week, the big house full of beds was half empty. And at the end of the second week, the last monkey had gotten well.

Then the Doctor's work was done, and he was so tired that he went to bed and slept for three days without even turning over.

Chee-Chee stood outside the Doctor's door, keeping everybody away till he woke up. Then John Dolittle told the monkeys that it was time for him to go home.

They were very surprised at this, for they had thought that he was going to stay with them forever. And that night all the monkeys got together in the jungle to talk it over.

The Chief Chimpanzee rose up and said, "Why is the good man going away? Is he not happy here with us?"

But none of them could answer him.

Then the Grand Gorilla got up and said,

"I think we all should ask him to stay. Perhaps if we make him a new house and a bigger bed, he will not wish to go."

Then Chee-Chee got up, and all the others whispered, "Shh! Look! Chee-Chee the Traveler is about to speak!"

And Chee-Chee said to the other monkeys, "My friends, I am afraid it is useless to ask the Doctor to stay. He owes money in Puddleby, and he says he must go back and pay it."

And the monkeys asked him, "What is money?"

Then Chee-Chee told them that in the land the Doctor came from, you could get nothing without money, you could do nothing without money — that it was almost impossible to *live* without money.

And some of them asked, "But can you not even eat and drink without paying?"

Chee-Chee shook his head.

The Chief Chimpanzee turned to the

Oldest Orangutan and said, "Cousin, these men are strange creatures! Who would wish to live in such a land?"

Then Chee-Chee said, "When we were coming to you, we had no boat to cross the sea in and no money to buy food to eat on our journey. So a man lent us some biscuits, and we said we would pay him when we came back. And we borrowed a boat from a sailor, but it was broken on the rocks when we reached the shores of Africa. Now the Doctor says he must go back and get the sailor another boat, because the man was poor and his ship was all he had."

The monkeys were all silent for a while, thinking hard.

At last, the Biggest Baboon got up and said, "I do not think we ought to let this good man leave our land till we have given him a fine present to take with him, so that he may know we are grateful for all that he has done for us."

A little, tiny red monkey who was sitting up in a tree shouted down, "I think that, too!"

And then they all cried out, making a loud noise, "Yes, yes. Let us give him the finest present a man has ever had!"

Now they began to wonder and ask one another what would be the best thing to give him. One said, "Fifty bags of coconuts!" And another, "A hundred bunches of bananas!"

But Chee-Chee told them that all these things would be too heavy to carry so far and would go bad before half of it was eaten.

"If you want to please him," he said, "give him an animal. You may be sure he will be kind to it. Give him some rare animal they have not got in the zoos."

And the monkeys asked him, "What are *zoos*?"

Then Chee-Chee explained to them that zoos were places where animals were put in cages for people to come and look at. And the monkeys were very shocked and said to one another, "These men are like thoughtless young ones — stupid and easily amused. Shh! It is a prison he means."

So then they asked Chee-Chee what rare animal they should give the Doctor — one he had not seen before. And the Major of the Marmosets asked, "Do they have an iguana over there?"

But Chee-Chee said, "Yes, there is one in the London Zoo."

And another asked, "Do they have an okapi?"

But Chee-Chee said, "Yes. In Belgium, in a big city they call Antwerp."

And another asked, "Do they have a pushmi-pullyu?"

Then Chee-Chee said, "No. No man outside of Africa has ever seen a pushmi-pullyu. Let us give him that."

The Ninth Chapter

The Rarest Animal of All

PUSHMI-PULLYUS are now extinct. That means there aren't any more. But long ago, when Doctor Dolittle was alive, there were still some left in the deepest jungles of Africa. Even then, they were very, very scarce. Pushmi-pullyus had no tail, but a head at each end, and sharp horns on each head. They were very shy and hard to catch.

Hunters got most of their animals by sneaking up behind them while they were not looking. But you could not do this with the pushmi-pullyu, because no matter which way you came toward him, he was always facing you. And besides, only one half of him slept at a time. The other head was always awake — and watching. This was why they were never caught and never seen in zoos. Though many of the greatest hunters spent years of their lives searching through the jungles for pushmi-pullyus, not a single one had ever been caught. Even then, years ago, it was the only animal in the world with two heads.

Well, the monkeys set out hunting for this animal through the forest. And after they had gone many miles, one of them found peculiar footprints near the edge of a river, and they knew that a pushmi-pullyu was very near that spot.

The monkeys went along the bank of the river a little way and they saw a place where the grass was high and thick, and they guessed that the pushmi-pullyu was in there. So they all joined hands and made a big circle around the high grass. The pushmi-pullyu heard them coming, and he tried hard to break through the ring of monkeys. But he couldn't do it.

When the pushmi-pullyu saw that it was no use trying to escape, he sat down and waited to see what they wanted.

The monkeys asked him if he would go with Doctor Dolittle and be put on show. But the pushmi-pullyu shook both his heads hard and said, "Certainly not!"

They explained to him that he would not be shut up in a zoo but would just be looked at. They told him that the Doctor was a very kind man who had no money. They explained that people would pay to see a two-headed animal, and the Doctor would get rich and could pay for the boat he had borrowed to come to Africa in.

But he answered, "No. You know how shy I am. I hate being stared at." And he almost began to cry.

For three days, they tried to persuade him. Finally, at the end of the third day, he said he would come with them and see what kind of a man the Doctor was.

So the monkeys traveled back with the

pushmi-pullyu. And when they came to the Doctor's little house of grass, they knocked on the door.

Dab-Dab, who was packing the trunk, said, "Come in!"

And Chee-Chee very proudly took the pushmi-pullyu inside and showed him to the Doctor.

"What in the world is this?" asked John Dolittle, gazing at the strange creature.

"Lord save us!" cried the duck. "How does it make up its mind?"

"It doesn't look to me as though it has one," said Jip, cocking his head.

"This, Doctor," said Chee-Chee, "is the pushmi-pullyu — the rarest animal of the African jungles and the only two-headed beast in the world! Take him home with you and your fortune's made. People will pay any money to see him."

"But I don't want any money," said the Doctor.

"Yes, you do," said Dab-Dab. "Don't

you remember how we had to pinch and scrape to pay the butcher's bill in Puddleby? And how are you going to get the sailor the new boat you promised unless we have the money to buy it?"

"I was going to make him one," said the Doctor.

"Oh, do be sensible!" cried Dab-Dab. "Where would you get all the wood and the nails to build it with? And besides, what are we going to live on? We shall be poorer than ever when we get back. Chee-Chee's perfectly right: Take the funny-looking thing along, do!"

"Well, perhaps there is something in what you say," murmured the Doctor. "He certainly would make a nice new kind of pet. But does the, er, what-do-you-call-it really want to go with us?"

"Yes, I'll go," said the pushmi-pullyu, who saw at once that the Doctor was a man to be trusted. "You have been so kind to the animals here — and the monkeys tell me that I am the only one who will do. But you must promise me that if I do not like it in your land, you will send me back."

"Why, certainly — of course, of course," said the Doctor. "Excuse me, surely you are related to the Deer Family, are you not?"

"Yes," said the pushmi-pullyu, "to the Abyssinian Gazelles and the Asiatic Chamois — on my mother's side. My father's great-grandfather was the last of the Unicorns."

"Most interesting!" murmured the Doctor.

"I notice," said Dab-Dab, "that you only talk with one of your mouths. Can't the other head talk as well?"

"Oh, yes," said the pushmi-pullyu. "But I keep the other mouth for eating, mostly. That way I can talk while I am eating without being rude. Our kind have always been very polite."

When the packing was finished, the monkeys gave a grand party for the Doctor, and all the animals of the jungle came. They had pineapples and mangoes and honey and all sorts of good things to eat and drink.

After they had all finished eating, the Doctor got up and said, "My friends. I am not clever at speaking long words after dinner, like some men. But I wish to tell you that I am very sad to be leaving your beautiful country. Because I have things to do in my own country, I must go. After I have gone, remember never to let the flies settle on your food before you eat it, and do not sleep on the ground when the rains are coming. I — er — er — I hope you will all live happily ever after."

When the Doctor stopped speaking and sat down, all the animals clapped for a long time, and the monkeys said to one another, "Let it be remembered always among our people that he sat and ate with us, here, under the trees. For surely he is the greatest of men!"

And the Grand Gorilla, who had the strength of seven horses in his hairy arms, rolled a huge rock up to the head of the table and said, "This stone will mark the spot forever."

And even to this day, in the heart of the jungle, that stone is still there. Monkey mothers, passing through the forest with their families, still point down at it from the branches and whisper to their children, "Shh! There it is — look — where the good doctor sat and ate food with us in the Year of the Great Sickness!"

When the party was over, the Doctor and his pets started out to go back to the seashore. And all the monkeys went with him as far as the edge of their country, carrying his trunk and bags, to see him off.

The Tenth Chapter

Prince Bumpo

BY the edge of the river, they stopped and said farewell. This took a long time, because all those thousands of monkeys wanted to shake John Dolittle's hand.

Afterward, when the Doctor and his pets were going on alone, Polynesia said, "We must tread softly and talk low as we go through the Land of the Jolliginki. If the King should hear us, he will send his soldiers to catch us again, for I am sure he is still very angry about the trick I played on him."

"What I am wondering," said the Doctor, "is where we are going to get another boat to go home in. Perhaps we'll find one that nobody is using lying about on the beach."

One day, while they were passing through a very thick part of the forest, Chee-Chee went ahead of them to look for coconuts. And while he was away, the Doctor and the rest of the animals got lost in the deep woods. They wandered around and around but could not find their way down to the seashore.

Chee-Chee was terribly upset when he could not find them. He climbed high trees and looked out from the top branches to try to see the Doctor's tall hat. He waved and shouted. He called to all the animals by name. But it was no use. They seemed to have disappeared.

Indeed, they had lost their way very badly. They had strayed a long way off the path, and the jungle was so thick with bushes and creepers and vines that sometimes they could hardly move at all, and the Doctor had to take out his pocket knife and cut his way along.

At last, after stumbling about for many days, getting their clothes torn and their faces covered with mud, they walked right into the King's back garden by mistake. The King's men came running and caught them right away.

But Polynesia flew into a tree in the garden, without anybody seeing her, and hid herself. The Doctor and the rest were taken before the King.

"Ha-ha!" cried the King. "So you are caught again! This time you shall not escape. Take them all back to prison and put double locks on the door. This man shall scrub my kitchen floor for the rest of his life!"

So the Doctor and his pets were led back to prison and locked up. And the Doctor was told that in the morning, he must begin scrubbing the kitchen floor.

They were all very unhappy.

"This is a nuisance," said the Doctor. "I really must get back to Puddleby."

All this time, Polynesia was still sitting in the tree in the palace garden. Soon, she spotted Chee-Chee swinging through the trees, still looking for the Doctor. When Chee-Chee saw her, he came into her tree and asked her what had become of the rest of them.

"The Doctor and all the animals have been caught by the King's men and locked up again," whispered Polynesia. "We lost our way in the jungle and ended up in the palace garden by mistake."

"But couldn't you guide them?" asked Chee-Chee, and he began to scold the parrot for letting them get lost while he was away looking for the coconuts.

"Shh!" said Polynesia. "Look! There's Prince Bumpo coming into the garden! He must not see us. Don't move, whatever you do!"

And there, sure enough, was Prince Bumpo, the King's son, opening the garden gate. He carried a book of fairy tales under his arm. He came strolling down the gravel walk, humming a sad song, till he reached a stone seat right under the tree where the parrot and the monkey were hiding. Then he lay down on the seat and began reading the fairy stories to himself.

Chee-Chee and Polynesia watched him, keeping very quiet and still.

After a while, the King's son laid the book down and sighed a weary sigh. "If I were only a *frog* prince!" he said with a dreamy, faraway look in his eyes.

Then Polynesia, talking in a small, high voice, said, "Bumpo, someone might turn thee into a frog prince one day."

The King's son started up off the seat and looked all around. "What is this I hear?" he cried. "The sweet music of a fairy's silver voice seems to ring from yonder branch! Strange!"

"Worthy Prince," said Polynesia, keeping very still so Bumpo couldn't see her, "you speak winged words of truth. For 'tis I, the Queen of the Fairies, who speaks to thee. I am hiding in a rosebud."

"Oh, tell me, Fairy Queen," cried Bumpo, clasping his hands in joy, "who is it that can turn me into a frog prince?"

"In thy father's prison," said the parrot, "there lies a famous wizard, John Dolittle by name. Many things he knows of medicine and magic, and mighty deeds has he performed. Yet the King, your father, has imprisoned him. Go to him, brave Bumpo, secretly, when the sun has set, and he shall make you the froggiest prince who ever won a fair lady! I have said enough. I must now go back to Fairyland. Farewell!"

"Farewell!" cried the Prince. "A thousand thanks, good Fairy Queen!"

And he sat down on the seat again with a smile upon his face, waiting for the sun to set.

The Eleventh Chapter

Medicine and Magic

VERY, very quietly, making sure that no one saw her, Polynesia slipped out behind the tree and flew across to the prison. She found Gub-Gub poking his nose through the bars of the window, trying to sniff the cooking smells that came from the palace kitchen. She told the pig to bring the Doctor to the window because she wanted to speak to him.

"Listen," whispered Polynesia when John Dolittle's face appeared. "Prince Bumpo is coming here tonight to see you. He thinks you are a great wizard, and you've got to find some way to turn him into a frog. But be sure to make him promise you first that he will open the prison door and find a ship for you."

"A *frog*?" said the Doctor. "Why on earth does he want to be a frog? And how am I to help him?"

"I don't know anything about that," said Polynesia impatiently. "But you *must* do it. You will think of a way. It is your only chance to get out of prison."

"Well, I suppose it *might* be possible," said the Doctor. "Let me see." And he went through his medicine bag, murmuring to himself.

Well, that night, Prince Bumpo went secretly to the Doctor in prison and said to him, "Great wizard, I am an unhappy prince. Years ago I went in search of a beautiful princess, like the ones in fairy tales. When at last I found one, I fell in love with her, and she with me. But she would not marry me! She said it was her destiny to kiss a frog who was really a prince, and make him her husband. Now I hear that you are a magician with many powerful potions. So I come to you for help. If you will turn me into a frog, so that I may win my beloved princess, I will give you half my kingdom and anything else you ask."

"Prince Bumpo," said the Doctor, looking thoughtfully at the bottles in his medicine bag, "suppose I taught you to speak in frog language — would that do to convince your princess?"

"That would be good," said Bumpo, "but not good enough. I must *look* like a frog as well."

"You know, it isn't so easy to change a man into a frog," said the Doctor. "That's one of the hardest things a magician can do. I can make your face look froglike, enough so that the princess will marry you. Will that do?"

"Yes, that will do," said Bumpo. "Because I shall wear shining armor and gauntlets of steel, like the princes in books, and ride on a horse."

"Well, I will do what I can for you," said the Doctor. "But before I do anything, you first must go down to the beach and prepare a ship to take me across the sea. And when I have done as you ask, you must let me and all my animals out of prison. Promise — by the Crown of Jolliginki!"

So the Prince promised and went away to get a ship ready.

When Bumpo came back and said that it was done, the Doctor spent an hour teaching him words in frog language. Then he asked Dab-Dab to bring a basin. He mixed a lot of medicines in the basin and told Bumpo to dip his face in it.

The Prince leaned down and put his face in, right up to his ears. He held it there a long time, so long that the Doctor got anxious and fidgety, standing first on one leg and then on the other, looking at all the bottles he had used for the mixture, and reading the labels on them again and again. A strong smell filled the prison, like the smell of paper burning.

At last, the Prince lifted his face up out of the basin, breathing very hard. And all the animals cried out in surprise.

The Prince's skin had turned a beautiful, bumpy green and brown, like lily pads on a muddy pond. It had a lovely froggy sheen to it, as well.

When John Dolittle lent him a little mirror to see himself in, he began dancing around the prison, croaking, "Will you marry me?" in frog language. But the Doctor asked him not to make so much noise, and to please open the prison door.

Bumpo begged to keep the mirror, as it was the only one in the Kingdom of Jolliginki, and he wanted to look at himself all day long. But the Doctor said he needed it to shave with.

Then the Prince, taking a bunch of copper keys from his pocket, undid the double locks. And the Doctor and all his animals ran as fast as they could down to the seashore, while Bumpo leaned against the wall of the empty dungeon, smiling after them happily, his big face shining like a wet banana leaf in the light of the moon.

When they came to the beach, they saw Polynesia and Chee-Chee waiting for them on the rocks near the ship.

"I feel sorry for Bumpo," said the Doctor. "I am afraid that the medicine I used won't last. Most likely he will look the same as ever very soon. But if he's lucky he'll stay green long enough to convince his princess to marry him. Poor Bumpo!"

"I don't believe he ever found a princess at all," said Jip. "He's just been reading too many fairy tales. Silly business!"

Then the pushmi-pullyu, Gub-Gub, Dab-Dab, Jip, and Too-Too went onto the ship with the Doctor. But Chee-Chee, Polynesia, and the crocodile stayed behind, because Africa was the land where they were born.

When the Doctor stood upon the boat, he looked over the side across the water. And then he remembered that they had no one with them to guide them back to Puddleby.

The wide, wide sea looked terribly big and lonesome in the moonlight, and he began to wonder if they would lose their way when they passed out of sight of land. But while he was wondering, they heard a strange whispering noise, high in the air, coming through the night. And the animals all stopped saying good-bye and listened.

The noise grew louder and bigger. It seemed to be coming nearer to them — a sound like the autumn wind blowing through the leaves of a poplar tree, or a heavy rain beating down upon a roof.

And Jip, with his nose pointing upward and his tail quite straight, said, "Birds! Millions of them, flying fast — that's it!"

And then they all looked up. And there, streaming across the face of the moon like a huge swarm of tiny ants, were thousands and thousands of little birds. Soon the whole sky seemed full of them, and still more kept coming — more and more. There were so many that they covered the whole moon so it could not shine, and the sea grew dark and black — like when a storm cloud passes over the sun.

And then all these birds came down close, skimming over the water and the land, and the night sky was left clear above, and the moon shone as before. The rustling of their feathers grew louder than ever. They began to settle on the sands, along the ropes of the ship — anywhere and everywhere except the trees. The Doctor could see that they had blue wings and white breasts and very short, feathered legs. As soon as they had all found a place to sit, suddenly, there was no noise left anywhere. All was quiet, all was still.

In the silent moonlight, John Dolittle spoke. "I had no idea that we had been in Africa so long. It will be nearly summer when we get home. For these are the swallows going back. Swallows, I thank you for waiting for us. Now we need not be afraid that we will lose our way upon the sea. Pull up the anchor and set the sail!"

When the ship moved out upon the water, those who stayed behind, Chee-Chee, Polynesia, and the crocodile, grew terribly sad. For never in their lives had they known anyone they liked as much as Doctor John Dolittle of Puddleby-on-the-Marsh.

The Twelfth Chapter

Red Sails and Blue Wings

SAILING homeward, the Doctor's ship had to pass the coast of Barbary. This coast is the seashore of the Great Desert. It is a wild, lonely place — all sand and stones. And it was here that the Barbary pirates lived.

These pirates, a bad lot of men, used to wait for sailors to be shipwrecked on their shores. And often, if they saw a boat passing, they would come out in their fast sailing ships and chase it. When they caught a boat like this at sea, they would steal everything on it, sink the ship, and sail back to Barbary singing songs and feeling proud of the mischief they had done. Then they used to make the people they had caught write home to their friends to ask for money. And if the friends sent no money, the pirates often threw the people into the sea.

Now, one sunshiny day, the Doctor and Dab-Dab were walking up and down on the ship for exercise. A nice fresh wind was blowing the boat along, and everybody was happy. Then Dab-Dab saw the sail of another ship a long way behind them on the edge of the sea. It was a red sail.

"I don't like the look of that sail," said Dab-Dab. "I have a feeling it isn't a friendly ship. I am afraid there is more trouble coming to us."

Jip, who was taking a nap in the sun, began to growl and talk in his sleep. "I smell roast beef cooking," he mumbled. "Underdone roast beef — with brown gravy over it."

"Good gracious!" cried the Doctor. "What's the matter with the dog? Is he *smelling* in his sleep as well as talking?"

"I suppose he is," said Dab-Dab. "All dogs can smell in their sleep."

"But what is he smelling?" asked the Doctor. "There is no roast beef cooking on our ship."

"No," said Dab-Dab. "The roast beef must be on that other ship over there."

"But that's ten miles away," said the Doctor. "He couldn't smell that far!"

"Oh, yes, he could," said Dab-Dab. "You ask him."

Then Jip, still fast asleep, began to growl again and his lip curled up angrily, showing his clean, white teeth. "I smell bad men," he growled, "the worst men I ever smelled. I smell trouble. I smell a fight — six bad scoundrels fighting against one brave man. *Woof — oo — woof!*" Then he barked loud, and woke himself up with a surprised look on his face.

"See!" cried Dab-Dab. "That boat is nearer now. You can count its three big sails — all red. Whoever they are, they are coming after us."

"They are bad sailors," said Jip, "and their ship is very swift. They are surely the pirates of Barbary."

"Well, we must put up more sails on our boat," said the Doctor, "so we can go faster and get away from them. Run downstairs, Jip, and fetch me all the sails you see."

The dog hurried downstairs and dragged up every sail he could find.

But even when all these were put up on the masts to catch the wind, the boat did not go nearly as fast as the pirates', which kept coming closer and closer.

"This is a poor ship the Prince gave us," said Gub-Gub. "We could sail faster in a soup bowl. Look how near they are now! You can see the mustaches on the faces of the men. There are six of them! What are we going to do?"

The Doctor asked Dab-Dab to fly up and tell the swallows that pirates were coming after them in a swift ship, and ask them what he should do about it.

When the swallows heard this, they all flew down to the Doctor's ship, and told him to unravel some pieces of long rope and make them into a lot of thin strings as quickly as he could. Then the ends of these strings were tied onto the front of the ship, and the swallows took hold of the strings with their feet and flew off, pulling the boat along.

And although swallows are not very strong when only one or two are by themselves, it is different when there are a lot of them together. And there, tied to the Doctor's ship, were a thousand strings. Two thousand swallows pulled on each string — all wonderfully swift fliers.

In a moment, the Doctor found himself traveling so fast that he had to hold his hat on with both hands, for he felt as though the ship itself were flying through waves that frothed and boiled with speed.

And all the animals on the ship began to laugh and dance about in the rushing air, for when they looked back at the pirates' ship, they could see that it was growing smaller now, instead of bigger. The red sails were being left far, far behind.

The Thirteenth Chapter

The Rats' Warning

DRAGGING a ship through the sea is hard work. After two or three hours, the swallows began to get tired and short of breath. They sent a message down to the Doctor to say that they would have to take a rest soon, and that they would pull the boat over to an island not far off, and hide it in a deep bay till they had the breath to go on.

And soon the Doctor saw the island they had spoken of. It had a very beautiful, tall, green mountain in the middle of it.

When the ship had sailed safely into the bay where it could not be seen from the open sea, the Doctor said he would go onto the island to look for water, because there was none left to drink on his ship. And he told all the animals to get out, too, and romp on the grass to stretch their legs.

Now, as they were getting off, the Doctor noticed that a whole lot of rats were coming up from downstairs and leaving the ship as well. Jip started to run after them, because chasing rats had always been his favorite game. But the Doctor told him to stop.

One big black rat, who seemed to want to say something to the Doctor, now crept forward timidly along the rail, watching the dog out of the corner of his eye. After he had coughed nervously two or three times, and cleaned his whiskers, and wiped his mouth, he said, "Ahem — er — you know, of course, that all ships have rats in them, Doctor, do you not?"

And the Doctor said, "Yes."

"And you have heard that rats always leave a sinking ship?"

"Yes," said the Doctor, "so I've been told."

"People," said the rat, "always speak of it with a sneer, as though it were something disgraceful. But you can't blame us, can you? After all, who *would* stay on a sinking ship, if he could get off it?"

"It's very natural," said the Doctor, "very natural. I quite understand. Is there — is there anything else you wish to say?"

"Yes," said the rat. "I've come to tell you that we are leaving this ship. But we wanted to warn you before we go. This is a bad ship you have here. It isn't safe. The sides aren't strong enough. Its boards are rotten. Before tomorrow night it will sink to the bottom of the sea."

"But how do you know?" asked the Doctor.

"We always know," answered the rat.

"The tips of our tails get that tingly feeling — like when your foot's asleep. It's a bad ship, Doctor. Don't sail in it anymore, or you'll surely be drowned. Good-bye! We are going to look for a good place to live on this island."

"Good-bye!" said the Doctor. "And thank you for telling me. Very considerate of you! Leave that rat alone, Jip! Come here! Lie down!"

So then the Doctor and all his animals went off, carrying pails and saucepans, to look for water on the island while the swallows took their rest.

"I wonder what this island is called," said the Doctor, as he was climbing up the mountainside. "It seems a pleasant place. What a lot of birds there are!"

"Why, these are the Canary Islands," said Dab-Dab. "Don't you hear the canaries singing?"

The Doctor stopped and listened. "Why, to be sure — of course!" he said.

"How stupid of me! I wonder if they can tell us where to find water."

The canaries, who had heard all about Doctor Dolittle from birds of passage, led him to a beautiful spring of cool, clear water, and they showed him lovely meadows where the birdseed grew, and all the other sights of their island.

The pushmi-pullyu was glad they had come, because he liked the green grass so much better than the dried apples he had been eating on the ship. And Gub-Gub squeaked for joy when he found a whole valley full of wild sugarcane.

A little later, when the doctor and his animals had all had plenty to eat and drink, and were lying on their backs while the canaries sang for them, two of the swallows came hurrying over, very flustered and excited.

"Doctor!" they cried. "The pirates have come into the bay, and they've all got onto your ship. They are downstairs looking for things to steal. They have left their own ship with nobody on it. If you hurry down to the shore, you can get onto their ship — which is very fast — and escape. But you'll have to be quick."

"That's a good idea," said the Doctor. "Splendid!"

And he called his animals together at once, said good-bye to the canaries, and ran down to the beach.

When they reached the shore, they saw the pirate ship, with the three red sails, standing in the water. Just as the swallows had said, there was nobody on it. All the pirates were downstairs in the Doctor's ship, looking for things to steal.

So John Dolittle told his animals to walk very softly, and they all crept onto the pirate ship.

The Fourteenth Chapter

The Barbary Dragon

EVERYTHING would have gone all right if Gub-Gub had not caught a cold while eating the damp sugarcane on the island. This is what happened:

After they had pulled up the anchor without a sound, and were moving the ship very, very carefully out of the bay, Gub-Gub suddenly sneezed so loudly that the pirates on the other ship came rushing upstairs to see what the noise was.

As soon as they saw that the Doctor was escaping, the pirates sailed right across the entrance to the bay so that the Doctor could not get out into the open sea.

Then the leader of these bad men

shook his fist at the Doctor and shouted across the water, "Ha-ha! You are caught, my fine friend! You were going to run off in my ship, eh? But you are not a good enough sailor to beat me, Ben Ali, the Barbary Dragon. I want that duck you've got — and the pig, too. We'll have pork chops and roast duck for supper tonight."

Poor Gub-Gub began to weep, and Dab-Dab got ready to fly to save her life. But Too-Too whispered to the Doctor, "Keep him talking, Doctor. Be pleasant to him. Our old ship is bound to sink soon. The rats said it would be at the bottom of the sea before tomorrow night, and the rats are never wrong. Keep him talking till the ship sinks under him."

"What, until tomorrow night?" said the Doctor. "Well, I'll do my best. Let me see. What shall I talk about?"

"Oh, let them attack," said Jip. "We can fight the dirty rascals. There are only six of them. I'd love to brag that I had bitten a real pirate. Let 'em come. We can fight them."

"But they have pistols and swords," said the Doctor. "No, that would never do. I must talk to him. Look here, Ben Ali —"

But before the Doctor could say any more, the pirates began to sail the ship nearer, laughing with glee, and saying to one another, "Who shall be the first to catch the pig?"

Poor Gub-Gub was dreadfully frightened, and the pushmi-pullyu began to sharpen his horns for a fight by rubbing them on the mast of the ship. Jip kept springing into the air and barking and calling Ben Ali bad names in dog language.

But then something seemed to go wrong with the pirates. They stopped laughing and cracking jokes. They looked puzzled. Something was making them uneasy.

Then Ben Ali, staring down at his feet,

suddenly bellowed out, "Thunder and lightning! Men, *the boat's leaking*!"

And then the other pirates peered over the side, and they saw that the boat was indeed getting lower and lower in the water. And one of them said to Ben Ali, "But surely if this old boat were sinking, we would see the rats leaving it."

And Jip shouted across from the other ship, "You fools, the rats left two hours ago! Ha-ha to you, my fine friends!"

But, of course, the men did not understand him. Soon the front end of the ship began to go down and down, faster and faster — till the boat looked almost as though it were standing on its head. The pirates had to cling to the rails and the masts and the ropes to keep from sliding off. Then the sea rushed roaring in through all the windows and the doors. And, at last, the ship plunged right down to the bottom of the sea, making a dreadful gurgling sound, and the six bad men were left bobbing about in the deep water of the bay.

Three of them started to swim for the shores of the island, while the others tried to get onto the boat where the Doctor was. But Jip kept snapping at their noses, so they were afraid to climb on board.

Then suddenly, they all cried out in fear, "The *sharks*! The sharks are coming! Let us get onto the ship before they eat us! Help, help! The sharks! The sharks!"

And now the Doctor could see, all over the bay, the backs of big fishes swimming swiftly through the water.

One big shark came near the ship and, poking his nose out of the water, he said to the Doctor, "Are you John Dolittle, the famous animal doctor?"

"Yes," said Doctor Dolittle. "That is my name."

"Well," said the shark, "we know these pirates to be a bad lot, especially Ben Ali. If they are annoying you, we will gladly eat them up for you, and then you won't be troubled anymore."

"Thank you," said the Doctor. "That is really most kind. But I don't think it will be necessary to eat them. Don't let any of them reach the shore until I tell you — just keep them swimming about, will you? And please make Ben Ali swim over here so that I may talk to him."

So the shark went off and chased Ben Ali over to the Doctor.

"Listen, Ben Ali," said John Dolittle, leaning over the side. "You have been a very bad man, and I understand that you have killed many people. These good sharks here have just offered to eat you up for me — and 'twould indeed be a good thing if the seas were rid of you. But if you will promise to do as I tell you, I will let you go in safety."

"What must I do?" asked the pirate, looking down sideways at the big shark who was smelling his leg under the water.

"You must kill no more people," said the Doctor. "You must stop stealing, you must never sink another ship, and you must give up being a pirate altogether."

"But what shall I do then?" asked Ben Ali. "How shall I live?"

"You and all your men must go onto this island and be birdseed farmers," the Doctor answered. "You must grow birdseed for the canaries."

The Barbary Dragon turned pale with anger. *"Grow birdseed!"* he groaned. "Can't I be a sailor?"

"No," said the Doctor, "you cannot. You have been a sailor long enough — and sent many strong ships and good men to the bottom of the sea. For the rest of your life, you must be a peaceful farmer. The shark is waiting. Make up your mind."

"Thunder and lightning!" Ben Ali muttered. *"Birdseed!"* Then he looked down into the water again and saw the big fish smelling his other leg.

"Very well," he said sadly. "We'll be farmers."

"And remember," said the Doctor, "that if you do not keep your promise — if you start killing and stealing again — I shall hear of it, because the canaries will come and tell me. And be very sure that I will find a way to punish you. I may not be able to sail a ship as well as you, but as long as the birds and the beasts and the fishes are my friends, I do not have to be afraid of a pirate chief — even if he calls himself the 'Barbary Dragon.' Now go and be a good farmer and live in peace."

Then the Doctor turned to the big shark and, waving his hand, he said, "All right. Let them swim safely to land."

The Fifteenth Chapter

Too-Too, the Listener

HAVING thanked the sharks again for their kindness, the Doctor and his pets set off once more on their journey home in the swift ship with the three red sails.

As they moved out into the open sea, the animals all went downstairs to see what their new boat was like inside. The Doctor leaned on the rail at the back of the ship, watching the Canary Islands fade away in the blue dusk of the evening.

While he was standing there, wondering how the monkeys were getting on — and what his garden would look like when he got back to Puddleby — Dab-Dab came tumbling up the stairs, all smiles and full of news.

100

"Doctor!" she cried. "This ship of the pirates is simply beautiful. The beds downstairs are made of silk, with hundreds of big pillows and cushions. There are thick, soft carpets on the floors, the dishes are made of silver, and there are all sorts of good things to eat and drink. You never saw anything like it in your life. Come and look. Oh, and we found a little room down there with the door locked, and we are all crazy to see what's inside. Jip says it must be where the pirates keep their treasure. But we can't open the door. Come down and see if you can let us in."

So the Doctor went downstairs, and he saw that it was indeed a beautiful ship. He found the animals gathered around a little door, all talking at once, trying to guess what was inside. The Doctor turned the handle but it wouldn't open. Then they all started to hunt for the key. They looked under the mat, they looked under the carpets, they looked in all the cupboards and drawers and lockers, and they looked in the big chests in the ship's dining room. They looked everywhere.

While they were doing this, they discovered a lot of new and wonderful things that the pirates must have stolen from other ships: Kashmir shawls as thin as a cobweb, embroidered with flowers of gold; jars of fine spices from Jamaica; carved ivory boxes full of Russian tea; an old violin with a string broken and a picture on the back; a set of big chessmen carved out of coral and amber; a walking stick that had a sword inside; six wineglasses with turquoise and silver around the rims; and a lovely, big sugar bowl made of mother of pearl. But nowhere in the whole boat could they find a key to fit that lock.

So they all went back to the door, and Jip peered through the keyhole. But something had been placed against the wall on the inside, and he could see nothing.

While they were standing around, wondering what they should do, Too-Too suddenly said, "Shh! Listen! I do believe there's someone in there!"

They all kept still a moment. Then the Doctor said, "You must be mistaken, Too-Too. I don't hear anything."

"I'm sure of it," said the owl. "Shh! There it is again! Don't you hear that?"

"No, I do not," said the Doctor. "What kind of a sound is it?"

"I hear the noise of someone putting his hand in his pocket," said the owl.

"But that makes hardly any sound at all," said the Doctor. "You couldn't hear that out here."

"Pardon me, but I can," said Too-Too. "I tell you there is someone on the other side of that door putting his hand in his pocket. Almost everything makes *some* noise — if your ears are only sharp enough to catch it. We owls can tell you, using only one ear, the color of a kitten from the way it winks in the dark."

"Well, well!" said the Doctor. "You surprise me. That's very interesting. Listen again and tell me what he's doing now."

"I'm not sure yet," said Too-Too, "if it's a man at all. Maybe it's a woman. Lift me up and let me listen at the keyhole, and I'll soon tell you."

So the Doctor lifted the owl up and held him close to the lock of the door.

After a moment, Too-Too said, "Now he's rubbing his face with his left hand. It is a small hand and a small face. It *might* be a woman. No. Now he pushes his hair back off his forehead. It's a man, all right."

"Women sometimes do that," said the Doctor.

"True," said the owl. "But when they do, their long hair makes quite a different sound. Shh! Make that fidgety pig keep still. Now all hold your breath a moment so I can listen well. The pesky door is so thick! Shh! Everybody be quite still — shut your eyes and don't breathe."

Too-Too leaned down and listened again very hard and long.

At last, he looked up into the Doctor's face and said, "The man in there is unhappy. He weeps. He has taken care not to blubber or sniffle, so we won't know he is crying. But I heard — quite distinctly — the sound of a tear falling on his sleeve."

"How do you know it wasn't a drop of water falling off the ceiling on him?" asked Gub-Gub.

"Pshaw!" sniffed Too-Too. "A drop of water falling off the ceiling would have made ten times as much noise!"

"Well," said the Doctor, "if the poor fellow's unhappy, we've got to get in and see what's the matter with him. Find me an ax, and I'll chop down the door."

The Sixteenth Chapter

The Ocean Gossips

RIGHT away, an ax was found. And the Doctor soon chopped a hole in the door big enough to clamber through.

At first he could see nothing at all, it was so dark inside. So he struck a match.

The room was quite small, with no window and a low ceiling. For furniture, there was only one little stool. All around the room, big barrels stood against the walls, fastened at the bottom so they wouldn't tumble with the rolling of the ship. Above the barrels, pewter jugs of all sizes hung from wooden pegs. There was a strong, winey smell. And in the middle of the floor sat a little boy, about eight years old, crying bitterly.

"I declare, it is the pirates' rum room!" said Jip in a whisper.

The little boy seemed frightened to find a man standing there before him and all those animals staring in through the hole in the broken door. But as soon as he saw John Dolittle's face by the light of the match, he stopped crying and stood up.

"You aren't one of the pirates, are you?" he asked.

And when the Doctor threw back his head and laughed long and loud, the little boy smiled and came and took his hand.

"You laugh like a friend," he said, "not like a pirate. Could you tell me where my uncle is?"

"I am afraid I can't," said the Doctor. "When did you see him last?"

"It was the day before yesterday," said the boy. "My uncle and I were out fishing in our little boat when the pirates came and caught us. They sunk our fishing boat and brought us both onto this ship. They told my uncle that they wanted him to be a pirate like them, for he was clever at sailing a ship in all weather. But he said he didn't want to be a pirate, because killing people and stealing isn't good work for a fisherman. Then the leader, Ben Ali, got very angry and gnashed his teeth, and said they would throw my uncle into the sea if he didn't do as they said. They sent me downstairs, and I heard the noise of a fight going on above. And when they let me come up again, my uncle was nowhere to be seen. I asked the pirates where he was, but they wouldn't tell me. I am very much afraid they threw him into the sea and drowned him." And the little boy began to cry again.

"Well now, wait a minute," said the Doctor. "Don't cry. Let's go and have tea in the dining room, and we'll talk it over. Maybe your uncle is quite safe. You don't *know* that he was drowned, do you? Perhaps we can find him for you. First, we'll go and have tea and toast with strawberry jam, and then we will see what can be done."

All the animals had been standing around listening. And when the boy and the Doctor had gone into the ship's dining room and were having tea, Dab-Dab came up behind the Doctor's chair and whispered, "Ask the porpoises if the boy's uncle was drowned — they'll know."

"All right," said the Doctor, taking a second piece of bread and jam.

"What are those funny clicking noises you are making with your tongue?" asked the boy.

"Oh, I just said a couple of words in duck language," the Doctor answered. "This is Dab-Dab, one of my pets."

"I didn't even know that ducks had a language," said the boy. "Are all these other animals your pets, too? What is that strange-looking thing with two heads?"

"Shh!" the Doctor whispered. "That is the pushmi-pullyu. Don't let him see that we're talking about him — he gets so dreadfully embarrassed. Tell me, how did you come to be locked up in that little room?"

"The pirates shut me in there when they were going off to steal things from another ship. When I heard someone chopping on the door, I didn't know who it could be. I was very glad to find it was you. Do you think you will be able to find my uncle for me?"

"Well, we are going to try very hard," said the Doctor. "Now what does your uncle look like?"

"He has red hair," the boy answered, "very red hair, and an anchor tattooed on his arm. He is a strong man, a kind uncle, and the best sailor in the south Atlantic. His fishing boat is called the *Saucy Sally*. It is a cutter-rigged sloop."

"What's 'cutterigsloop'?" whispered Gub-Gub, turning to Jip.

"Shh! That's the kind of ship the man had," said Jip. "Keep still, can't you?"

The Doctor left the boy to play with the animals in the dining room, and went upstairs to look for passing porpoises. And soon a whole school came dancing and jumping through the water, on their way to Brazil. The Doctor asked them if they had seen anything of a man with red hair and an anchor tattooed on his arm.

"Do you mean the master of the *Saucy Sally*?" asked the porpoises.

"Yes," said the Doctor. "That's the man. Has he been drowned?"

"His fishing sloop was sunk," said the porpoises, "for we saw it lying on the bottom of the sea. But there was nobody inside it, because we went and looked."

"His little nephew is on the ship with me here," said the Doctor. "And he is terribly afraid that the pirates threw his uncle into the sea. Would you be so good as to find out for me, for sure, whether he has been drowned or not?"

"Oh, he isn't drowned," said the porpoises. "If he were, we would be sure to have heard of it from the deep-sea crabs. We hear all the saltwater news. The shellfish call us 'the ocean gossips.' No — tell the little boy we are sorry we do not know where his uncle is, but we are quite certain he hasn't been drowned in the sea."

So the Doctor ran downstairs and told the nephew, who clapped his hands with happiness. And the pushmi-pullyu took the little boy on his back and gave him a ride around the dining room table. All the other animals followed behind, beating the pots and pans with spoons, pretending it was a parade.

The Seventeenth Chapter

Smells

"YOUR uncle must now be *found*," said the Doctor. "That is the next thing, now that we know he wasn't thrown into the sea."

Then Dab-Dab came up to him again and whispered, "Ask the eagles to look for the man. No living creature can see better than an eagle. When they are miles high in the air, they can count the ants crawling on the ground. Ask the eagles."

So the Doctor sent one of the swallows to get some eagles.

And in about an hour, the little bird came back with six different kinds of eagles: a black eagle, a bald eagle, a fish eagle, a golden eagle, an eagle-vulture, and a white-tailed sea eagle. Each was twice as tall as the boy. They stood on the rail of the ship, like round-shouldered soldiers all in a row, stern and still and stiff. Their gleaming black eyes shot darting glances here and there and everywhere.

Gub-Gub was scared of them and hid behind a barrel. He said he felt as though their terrible eyes were looking right inside of him to see what he had eaten for lunch.

The Doctor said to the eagles, "A man has been lost — a fisherman with red hair and an anchor marked on his arm. Would you be so kind as to see if you can find him for us? This boy is the man's nephew."

Eagles do not talk very much. And all they said in their husky voices was, "You may be sure that we will do our best for John Dolittle." Then they flew off.

Gub-Gub came out from behind his barrel to see them go. Up and up and up they went, higher and higher and higher still. Then, when the Doctor could barely see them, they parted company and started off in all directions — north, east, south, and west, looking like tiny grains of black sand creeping across the wide, blue sky.

They were gone a long time. And when they came back, it was almost night.

And the eagles said to the Doctor, "We have searched all the seas and all the countries and all the islands and all the cities and all the villages in this half of the world. But we have failed. Nowhere, on land or water, could we see any sign of this boy's uncle. And if *we* could not see him, then he is not to be seen. For John Dolittle, we have done our best." Then the six giant birds flapped their big wings and flew back to their homes in the mountains and the rocks.

"Well," said Dab-Dab, after they had gone, "what are we going to do now? The boy's uncle *must* be found — there's no two ways about that. Boys aren't like ducklings — they have to be taken care of till they're quite old. I wish Chee-Chee were here. He would soon find the man. Good old Chee-Chee! I wonder how he's doing!"

"If we only had Polynesia with us," said Too-Too. "*She* would soon think of some way. My, but she was a clever one!"

"I don't think so much of those eagle fellows," said Jip. "They may have good eyesight, but when you ask them to find a man for you, they can't do it — and they have the cheek to say that *nobody* could do it. And I don't think a whole lot of those gossipy old porpoises, either. All they could tell us was that the man isn't in the sea. We don't want to know where he *isn't* — we want to know where he *is*."

"Oh, don't talk so much," said Gub-Gub. "It's easy to talk, but it isn't so easy to find a man when you have the whole world to hunt him in. You don't know everything. You're just talking. You couldn't find the boy's uncle any more than the eagles could."

"Couldn't I?" said Jip. "That's all you know! I haven't begun to try yet, have I? You wait and see!"

Then Jip went to the Doctor and said, "Ask the boy if he has anything in his pockets that belonged to his uncle, will you, please?"

So the Doctor asked him. And the boy showed them a gold ring that he wore on a piece of string around his neck because it was too big for his finger. He said his uncle gave it to him when they saw the pirates coming.

Jip smelled the ring and said, "That's no good. Ask him if he has anything else that belonged to his uncle."

Then the boy took from his pocket a great, big red handkerchief and said, "This was my uncle's, too."

As soon as the boy pulled it out, Jip shouted, "*Snuff*, by jingo! Black rappee snuff. Don't you smell it? His uncle took snuff! Ask him, Doctor."

The Doctor questioned the boy again, and he said, "Yes. My uncle took a lot of snuff. He liked the way it made him sneeze."

"Fine!" said Jip. "The man's as good as found. Tell the boy I'll find his uncle for him in less than a week. Let us go upstairs and see which way the wind is blowing."

"But it is dark now," said the Doctor. "You can't find him in the dark!"

"I don't need any light to look for a man who smells of black rappee snuff," said Jip as he climbed the stairs. "If the man had a hard smell, like string, or hot water, it would be different. But *snuff*! Tut, tut!"

"Does hot water have a smell?" asked the Doctor.

"Certainly it has," said Jip. "Hot water smells quite different from cold water. Why, I once followed a man for ten miles on a dark night by the smell of the hot water he had bathed in. Now then, let us see which way the wind is blowing. Wind is very important in long-distance smelling. It mustn't be too fierce a wind — and, of course, it must blow the right way. A nice, steady, damp breeze is the best of all. Ha! This wind is from the north."

Then Jip went up to the front of the ship and smelled the wind, and he started muttering to himself, "Tar, Spanish onions, kerosene oil, wet raincoats, crushed laurel leaves, burning rubber, lace curtains being washed — no, my mistake — lace curtains hanging out to dry, and foxes — hundreds of 'em — cubs, and —"

"Can you really smell all those things in the wind?" asked the Doctor.

"Why, of course!" said Jip. "And those are only the easy smells — the strong ones. Wait now, and I'll tell you some of the harder scents that are coming on this wind — a few of the dainty ones."

Then the dog shut his eyes tight, poked

his nose straight up in the air, and sniffed hard with his mouth half open.

For a long time he said nothing. He was as still as a stone. He hardly seemed to be breathing at all. When at last he began to speak, it sounded almost as though he were singing, sadly, in a dream.

"Bricks," he whispered, very low, "old yellow bricks, crumbling with age in a garden wall; the sweet breath of young cows standing in a mountain stream; the lead roof of a pigeon roost — or perhaps a grain shed — with the midday sun on it; black kid gloves lying in a bureau drawer of walnut wood; a dusty road with a horses' drinking trough beneath the sycamores; little mushrooms bursting through the rotting leaves; and — and — and —"

"Any parsnips?" asked Gub-Gub.

"No," said Jip. "You always think of things to eat. No parsnips whatever. And no snuff. We must wait till the wind changes to the south."

"I think you're a fake, Jip," said Gub-Gub. "Who ever heard of finding a man in the middle of the ocean just by smell! I told you you couldn't do it."

"Look here," said Jip, getting really angry. "You're going to get a bite on the nose in a minute!"

"Stop quarreling!" said the Doctor. "Stop it! Life's too short. Let's go down to supper. I'm quite hungry."

"So am I," said Gub-Gub.

The Eighteenth Chapter

The Rock

UP they got, early the next morning, out of the silken beds, and they saw that the sun was shining brightly and that the wind was blowing from the south.

Jip smelled the south wind for half an hour. Then he came to the Doctor, shaking his head. "I smell no snuff yet," he said. "We must wait till the wind changes to the east."

But even when the east wind came that afternoon, the dog could not catch the smell of snuff.

The little boy was terribly disappointed and began to cry again, saying that no one seemed to be able to find his uncle for him. But all Jip said to the Doctor was,

"Tell him that when the wind changes to the west, I'll find his uncle even if he is in China — as long as he is still taking black rappee snuff."

Three days they had to wait before the west wind came. This was on a Friday morning, early — just as it was getting light. A fine rainy mist lay on the sea like a thin fog. And the wind was soft and warm and wet.

As soon as Jip awoke, he ran upstairs and poked his nose in the air. Then he got very excited and rushed down again to wake the Doctor up.

"Doctor!" he cried. "I've got it! Doctor! Doctor! Wake up! Listen! I've got it! The wind is from the west and it smells of nothing but snuff. Come upstairs and turn the ship — quick!"

So the Doctor tumbled out of bed and went to the rudder to steer the ship.

"Now I'll go up to the front," said Jip, "and you watch my nose. Whichever way I point it, steer the ship the same way. The man cannot be far off, with the smell as strong as this. And the wind's all lovely and wet. Now watch me!"

So all that morning, Jip stood in the front part of the ship, sniffing the wind and pointing the way for the Doctor to steer. All the animals and the little boy stood around with their eyes wide open, watching the dog in wonder.

About lunchtime, Jip asked Dab-Dab to tell the Doctor that he was getting worried and wanted to speak to him. So Dab-Dab went and fetched the Doctor from the other end of the ship and Jip said to him, "The boy's uncle is starving. We must make the ship go as fast as we can."

"How do you know he is starving?" asked the Doctor.

"Because there is no other smell in the west wind but snuff," said Jip. "If the man were cooking or eating food of any kind, I would be bound to smell it, too. But he doesn't even have freshwater to drink. All he is taking is snuff — in large pinches. We are getting nearer to him all the time, because the smell grows stronger every minute. Make the ship go as fast as you can."

"All right," said the Doctor, and he sent Dab-Dab to ask the swallows to pull the ship again.

So the little birds came down once more and harnessed themselves to the ship.

And now the boat went bounding through the waves at a terrible speed. It went so fast that the fishes in the sea had to jump for their lives to get out of the way and not be run over.

And all the animals got tremendously excited, and they gave up looking at Jip and turned to watch the sea in front, to spy any land or islands where the starving man might be.

But hour after hour went by and still

the ship went rushing on, over the same flat, flat sea, and no land anywhere came in sight.

And now the animals gave up chattering and sat around silent, anxious, and miserable. The little boy grew sad again. And on Jip's face, there was a worried look.

At last, late in the afternoon, just as the sun was going down, Too-Too, who was perched on the tip of the mast, startled them all by crying out at the top of his voice, "Jip! Jip! I see a giant rock in front of us. Look — way out there where the sky and the water meet. Is the smell coming from there?"

And Jip called back, "Yes. That's it. That is where the man is. At last, at last!"

And when they got nearer, they could see that the rock was very large — as large as a big field. No trees grew on it, no grass — nothing. The rock was as smooth and as bare as the back of a tortoise.

Then the Doctor sailed the ship all

around the rock. But they didn't see a man anywhere. All the animals screwed up their eyes and looked as hard as they could, and John Dolittle got a telescope from downstairs.

But not one living thing could they spy — not even a gull, nor a starfish, nor a shred of seaweed.

They all stood still and listened, straining their ears for any sound. But the only noise they heard was the gentle lapping of the little waves against the sides of their ship.

Then they all started calling, "Hello, there! *Hello!*" till their voices were hoarse. But only the echo came back from the rock.

And the little boy burst into tears and said, "I am afraid I shall never see my uncle again! What shall I tell them when I get home?"

But Jip called to the Doctor, "He must be there. He must — *he must!* The smell goes on no farther. Sail the ship close to the rock and let me jump out on it."

So the Doctor brought the ship as close as he could and let down the anchor. Then he and Jip got out of the ship and went onto the rock.

Jip put his nose down close to the ground and began to run all over the place. Up and down he went, back and forth — zigzagging, twisting, doubling, and turning. And everywhere he went, the Doctor ran behind him, close at his heels, till he was terribly out of breath.

At last, Jip let out a loud bark and sat down. And when the Doctor came running up to him, he found the dog staring into a big, deep hole in the middle of the rock.

"The boy's uncle is down there," said Jip quietly. "No wonder those silly eagles couldn't see him! It takes a dog to find a man."

So the Doctor got down into the hole,

which seemed to be a kind of cave or tunnel running a long way under the ground. Then he struck a match and started to make his way along the dark passage with Jip following behind.

The Doctor's match soon went out, and he had to strike another and another and another.

At last the passage came to an end, and the Doctor found himself in a kind of tiny room with walls of rock.

And there, in the middle of the room, his head resting on his arms, lay a man with very red hair — fast asleep!

Jip went up and sniffed at something lying on the ground beside him. The Doctor stooped and picked it up. It was an enormous snuffbox. And it was full of black rappee!

The Nineteenth Chapter

The Fisherman's Town

GENTLY then — very gently, the Doctor woke the man up.

But just at that moment, the match went out again. And the man thought it was Ben Ali coming back, and he began to punch the Doctor in the dark.

But when John Dolittle told him who it was, and that he had his little nephew safe on his ship, the man was tremendously glad, and said he was sorry.

And the man told how the Barbary Dragon had left him on that rock when he wouldn't promise to become a pirate, and how he had been sleeping down in that hole to keep warm.

And then he said, "For four days I have

had nothing to eat or drink. I have lived on snuff."

"There you are!" said Jip. "What did I tell you?"

So they struck some more matches and made their way out through the passage into the daylight, and the Doctor hurried the man onto the boat to get some soup.

When the animals and the little boy saw the Doctor and Jip coming back to the ship with a red-headed man, they began to cheer and yell. And the swallows up above started whistling at the top of their voices to show that they, too, were glad. The noise they made was so loud that sailors far out at sea thought that a terrible storm was coming. "Hark to that gale howling in the east!" they said.

And Jip was awfully proud of himself — though he tried hard not to show it. When Dab-Dab said, "Jip, I had no idea you were so clever!" he just tossed his head and answered, "Oh, that's nothing special.

But it takes a dog to find a man, you know. Birds are no good for a game like that."

Then the Doctor asked the red-haired fisherman where his home was. And when he had told him, the Doctor asked the swallows to guide the ship there first.

And when they came to the land that the man had spoken of, they saw a little fishing town at the foot of a rocky mountain, and the man pointed out the house where he lived.

And while they were letting down the anchor, the little boy's mother (who was also the man's sister) came running down to the shore to meet them, laughing and crying at the same time. She had been sitting on a hill for twenty days, watching the sea and waiting for them to return.

She kissed the Doctor many times, so that he giggled and blushed like mad. And she tried to kiss Jip, too, but he ran away and hid inside the ship.

The fisherman and his sister didn't want

the Doctor to go away in a hurry. They begged him to spend a few days with them.

And all the little boys of the fishing village went down to the beach and pointed at the ship anchored there, and said to one another in whispers, "Look! That was the ship of Ben Ali — the most terrible pirate that ever sailed the seven seas! That funny gentleman with the tall hat, *he* took the ship from the Barbary Dragon and made him into a farmer."

During the two and a half days that the Doctor stayed at the little fishing town, the people kept asking him out to teas and luncheons and dinners and parties. All the ladies sent him boxes of flowers and candies, and the village band played tunes under his window every night.

At last the Doctor said, "Good people, I must go home now. You really have been most kind. I shall always remember it. But I must go home, for I have things to do."

Then, just as the Doctor was about to leave, the Mayor of the town came down the street and stopped before the house where the Doctor was staying. Everybody in the village gathered around to see what was going to happen.

After six pageboys had blown on shining trumpets to make the people stop talking, the Doctor came out onto the steps and the Mayor spoke. "Doctor John Dolittle," said he. "It is a great pleasure for me to present to the man who rid the seas of the Barbary Dragon this little token from the grateful people of our worthy town."

The Mayor took from his pocket a little tissue-paper packet, and opening it, he handed to the Doctor a perfectly beautiful watch with real diamonds in the back.

Then the Mayor pulled a larger parcel out of his pocket and said, "Where is the dog?"

Then everybody started to hunt for Jip. At last, Dab-Dab found him on the other side of the village in a stable yard, where all the dogs of the countryside were standing around him speechless with admiration and respect.

When Jip was brought to the Doctor's side, the Mayor opened the larger parcel, and inside was a dog collar made of solid gold! A murmur of wonder went up from the village folk as the Mayor bent down and fastened it around the dog's neck.

For written on the collar in big letters were these words: JIP — THE CLEVEREST DOG IN THE WORLD.

Then the whole crowd moved down to the beach to see them off. And after the red-haired fisherman and his sister and the little boy had thanked the Doctor and his dog over and over and over again, the swift ship with the red sails was turned once more toward Puddleby, and they sailed out to sea, while the village band played music on the shore.

The Last Chapter

Home Again

MARCH winds had come and gone, April's showers were over, May's buds had opened into flowers, and the June sun was shining on the pleasant fields, when John Dolittle, at last, got back to his own country.

But he did not yet go home to Puddleby. First, he went traveling through the land with the pushmi-pullyu in a gypsy wagon, stopping at all the country fairs. And there, with the acrobats on one side of them and the Punch and Judy show on the other, they would hang out a big sign which read, COME AND SEE THE MARVELOUS TWO-HEADED ANIMAL FROM THE JUNGLES OF AFRICA. ADMISSION: SIXPENCE.

And the pushmi-pullyu would stay inside the wagon, while the other animals would lie underneath. The pushmi-pullyu soon got used to people looking at him, and even began to like it when they oohed and aahed and said how wonderful and exotic he was. The Doctor sat in a chair in front taking the sixpences and smiling at the people as they went in, and Dab-Dab was kept busy all the time scolding him because he let the children in for nothing when she wasn't looking.

And zookeepers and circus men came and asked the Doctor to sell them the strange creature, saying they would pay a tremendous amount of money for him. But the Doctor always shook his head and said, "No. The pushmi-pullyu shall never be shut up in a cage. He shall be free always to come and go, like you and me."

It was very interesting at first, being sort of part of a circus, but after a few weeks, they all got dreadfully tired of it, and the

Doctor and his animals were longing to go home. And so many people came flocking to the little wagon and paid the sixpence to go inside and see the pushmi-pullyu that very soon the Doctor was able to give up being a showman.

One fine day, when the hollyhocks were in full bloom, he went back to Puddleby a rich man, to live in the little house with the big yard.

And the old lame horse in the stable was glad to see him, and so were the swallows who had already built their nests under the eaves of his roof and had young ones. And Dab-Dab was glad, too, to get back to the house she knew so well — although there was a terrible lot of dusting to be done, with cobwebs everywhere.

After Jip had gone and shown his golden collar to the other dogs in the neighborhood, he came back and began running around the garden like a crazy thing, looking for the bones he had buried long ago, and chasing the rats out of the toolshed. Gub-Gub dug up the horserad-ish that had grown three feet tall in the corner by the garden wall.

And the Doctor went and saw the sailor who had lent him the boat, and he bought two new ships for him and a doll for his baby, and he paid the grocer for the food he had lent him for the journey to Africa. And he bought another piano and put the white mice back in it, because they said the bureau drawer was drafty.

Even when the Doctor had filled the old money box on the dresser shelf, he still had a lot of money left, and he had to get three more money boxes, just as big, to put the rest in.

"Money," he said, "is a terrible nui-sance. But it's nice not to have to worry."

"Yes," said Dab-Dab, who was toasting muffins for his tea, "it is, indeed!"

And when the winter came again, and the snow flew against the kitchen window, the Doctor and his animals would sit around the big, warm fire after supper, and he would read aloud to them out of his books.

But far away in Africa, where the monkeys chattered in the palm trees before they went to bed under the big yellow moon, they would say to one another, "I wonder what the good man's doing now! Do you think he ever will come back?"

And Polynesia would squeak out from the vines, "I think he will — I guess he will — I hope he will!"

And then the crocodile would grunt up at them from the black mud of the river, "I'm *sure* he will. Go to sleep!"